Jump, Frog, Jump!

by Robert Kalan

pictures by Byron Barton

Greenwillow Books, New York

For my brother Bill, with love
Text copyright © 1981 by Robert Kalan. Illustrations copy-
right © 1981 by Byron Barton. First published in 1981 by
Greenwillow Books; reissued in 1995. All rights reserved.
No part of this book may be reproduced without permission
in writing from the Publisher, Greenwillow Books, a division
of William Morrow & Company, Inc., 1350 Avenue of the
Americas, New York, NY 10019. Printed in Singapore by
Tien Wah Press.   First Edition   10 9 8 7 6 5 4 3 2
The Library of Congress cataloged an earlier version of this
title as follows: Kalan, Robert.   Jump, frog, jump!
Summary: A cumulative tale in which a frog tries to catch
a fly without getting caught itself.   [1. Stories in rhyme]
I. Barton, Byron.   II. Title.   PZ8.3.K1246Ju   [E]
81-1401   ISBN 0-688-80271-0   AACR2
ISBN 0-688-84271-2 (lib. bdg.)
New edition: ISBN 0-688-13954-X

This is the fly that climbed out of the water.

This is the frog that was under the fly
that climbed out of the water.

How did the frog catch the fly?

Jump, frog, jump!

This is the fish that swam after the frog

that was under the fly

that climbed out of the water.

How did the frog get away?

Jump, frog, jump!

This is the snake that dropped from a branch

and swallowed the fish

that swam after the frog

that was under the fly that climbed out of the water.

How did the frog get away?

Jump, frog, jump!

This is the turtle that slid into the pond

and ate the snake that dropped from a branch

and swallowed the fish

that swam after the frog

that was under the fly that climbed out of the water.

How did the frog get away?

Jump, frog, jump!

This is the net that wrapped around the turtle

that slid into the pond and ate the snake

that dropped from a branch

and swallowed the fish

that swam after the frog

that was under the fly that climbed out of the water.

How did the frog get away?

Jump, frog, jump!

These are the kids who picked up the net

that wrapped around the turtle

that slid into the pond and ate the snake

that dropped from a branch

and swallowed the fish

that swam after the frog

that was under the fly that climbed out of the water.

How did the frog get away?

Jump, frog, jump!

This is the basket put over the frog

by the kids who picked up the net

that wrapped around the turtle

that slid into the pond and ate the snake

that dropped from a branch

and swallowed the fish

that swam after the frog

that was under the fly that climbed out of the water.

How did the frog get away?